THE GOLDSMITH'S
SECRET

Also by Elia Barceló in English translation

Heart of Tango (2010)

ELIA BARCELÓ

THE GOLDSMITH'S
SECRET

Translated from the Spanish by
David Frye

MACLEHOSE PRESS
QUERCUS · LONDON

The moral right of Elia Barceló to be
identified as the author of this work has been
asserted in accordance with the Copyright,
Designs and Patents Act, 1988.

David Frye asserts his moral right to be identified as
the translator of the work.

A CIP catalogue record for this book is available
from the British Library.

ISBN 978 0 85705 005 2

This book is a work of fiction. Names, characters,
businesses, organizations, places and events are
either the product of the author's imagination
or are used fictitiously. Any resemblance to
actual persons, living or dead, events or
locales is entirely coincidental.

10 9 8 7 6 5 4 3 2 1

Designed and typeset in Albertina by Libanus Press, Marlborough
Printed and bound in Great Britain by Clays Ltd, St Ives plc

To Mr Leonard Cohen,
whose songs have kept me going
throughout my life.
Thank you for the songs!

THE GOLDSMITH'S
SECRET

4.00 a.m. End of December.

Here I sit, writing for myself, by hand, in my minute goldsmith's lettering, in this recently rented, half empty flat. Beyond the window, snow falls docile on Clinton Street, where the music of which Leonard Cohen spoke is no longer to be heard. Writing for myself. There is no-one else to write for. No-one. Now that Celia is no more.

I have smoked three cigarettes trying to find the right words, how to begin, a starting point for the story I will tell today. But where will I find it? How? How, if it has no beginning? If its end – the end that set its stamp on my life so many years ago – came just six days before today's cold New York dawn?

Memories crowd in, furiously struggling to impose themselves on the disorder of my mind, but they meld into a glassy magma through which I can barely glimpse the outlines of what once was.

A possible beginning. It was September, a windy night, fore-boding storms. I had nodded off in the empty compartment of the train that was to convey me to Oneira, where I was going to say goodbye to Uncle Eloy – my only remaining relative, the one who taught me my trade, the one who gave me a place in his watch shop when I left Villasanta at the age of twenty, desperate, vowing never to return.

The aisle light spread a faint glow over my face. Its ghostly reflection in the compartment window brought back to my mind a face that had vanished for ever when I left, the face that I had once had as a child, as if the child that I had been back then were simply hiding somewhere inside me, waiting for some slip on my part to emerge from the muddy waters of the past with his happy smile and twinkling eyes. Twenty-five years had passed since I had left Villasanta de la Reina, leaving behind everything that had been my life up to that point, leaving behind school, friends, dances, strolls through the town square. Leaving Celia behind.

I remember that I then recalled, with an intensity that made me sit bolt upright in my seat, frightened by my own memory, the precise instant when I met her: her dark profile in the lobby of the Lys, the tiny pearl in her ear, the white handkerchief with which she dabbed delicately at her eyelashes while leaving the cinema, her quick glance at the girlfriend who reassured her with a smile, saying, "Don't worry, it doesn't show at all." It was as if my heart could not decide, as if it wanted to stop beating altogether and at the same time to run away at a gallop, drawn to that woman, so frail yet so hard, like a *film noir* actress in her tailored dress and pearl necklace, like a fallen star that had landed in the mud of our local cinema, the floor strewn with sunflower-seed husks and greasy tuna pastry wrappers. It was then that I learned that she was called the black widow. That was what Tony told me, with an elbow in my ribs, as she slipped into the crowd streaming from the late night film.

I left the cinema in a trance, resolved to do whatever it took to see her again, to get her to look at me, to hear her voice. I did not even notice that my friends had dragged me into Negresco's for a drink before heading home. It was only when we were sitting at the table at the back, under the mirror, that I realized the waiter was standing there and growing impatient. I mumbled, "Coffee with milk," but after Fabián left, in the space where his dazzlingly white apron had blinded me seconds earlier, I saw her, right in front of me, standing in the middle of the café, staring at me with an expression that I could not decipher, something that oscillated between surprise, joy and terror, something that I would only understand twenty-five years later, when it was too late.

She stood stock-still, just feet from us, gripping the handle of her bag as if her life depended on it. Her girlfriend approached us, fussy and lively, with the ridiculous flirtatiousness of an old maid of forty-something who always gets what she wants. "Kids, hope you don't mind. There are plenty of empty tables, and we always sit here. Fabián must have forgotten to tell you. You don't mind, do you? Celia likes this table."

I stood up right away. I would have crawled off on my knees if she had asked me. My friends, good sorts, were also standing up and making gestures to the bar that they should bring our drinks to the other table. "Old ladies and their fancies, what are you going to do?" Celia did not look like an old lady to me. Her skin was pale, creamy, soft; slight wrinkles around eyes that never looked away from mine, eyes that I thought then were the colour of beer and that only later, after I had become a goldsmith, would I compare to Brazilian topaz, crystallized beams of the setting sun.

Memories bustled and bumped up against my closed eyelids, like a crowd leaving an enormous cinema through a single exit door, pushing, shoving, jostling one another, ceding ground to the more daring or less cautious among them, tumbling out across the threshold one after another. Images I had thought long forgotten appeared for a few dazzling seconds before giving way to others just as intense, just as finely detailed: Saturday strolls along Jardines Street; summer dances in the club garden, decorated for the annual fiesta; endless conversations at Negresco's with my school-mates, imagining our always brilliant, always triumphant futures; sneaking our first cigarettes behind the cemetery wall; going for a dip in the river; catching a glimpse of the new primary school teacher in her slip, in the house that

Remedios the midwife had rented to her and that still had no blinds, to the scandal of the neighbours who ultimately gave her a set of curtains for her bedroom as a present; the oily tuna sandwiches we bought from Florinda, the old lady who ran the boarding house, married to a lazy fellow who came to a bad end in some hovel in Montecaín.

Smells, sounds, lights, for ever lost in the bogs of memory, along with recollections of my childhood home, boarded up by my parents when they moved to Oneira after my sister died at the age of twenty-two, run over by a motorcycle on a Paris street on the last day of summer courses. The house that, with my parents now also dead, would still be standing in Villasanta, furniture covered in dust, ageing photographs stacked away in boxes, the everyday cutlery in the kitchen, the sheets gnawed perhaps by mice; the house whose keys I had carried with me like a strange amulet ever since my father's death, never planning to use them.

The train rumbled through the second of three tunnels that, like a muttered "Open Sesame", reveal the entrance to Umbría, "Land of Legends", as our tourist slogan puts it. Before passing through the third tunnel, before I knew what I was doing or why, I pulled down my two suitcases, all the luggage that was coming with me on my move to New York, put on my raincoat, and stood on the platform of the car, waiting to round the long curve and watch the station for Villasanta de la Reina appear.

I do not know what I was thinking. I do not know what I expected to find. I only knew that something inside me was repeating "Now or never," and remember knowing that if I let this chance go by, if I stayed on the train to Oneira, I would go on to take the charter flight to London, then the flight to New York, and I would never see my childhood town again.

The train pulled into the station that I had not seen since 1974. For a moment I was about to close the door again, but instead I set my foot on the passenger step, swung down my suitcases, and stepped down on to the platform, holding my hat down with one hand and reading the large brown letters above the wrought-iron pergola, while at my back I heard the train start up again. When I turned around, all I saw were red lights disappearing into darkness. No-one else had got off. The station master, lamp in hand, shielding his face from the wind, asked me, in the Umbrilian accent I had almost forgotten, "Will you be going down to town?"

I nodded.

He went on, "I'll let Braulio know, if you'd like. Or perhaps someone's expecting you?"

"No," I said. "No-one is expecting me."

I lit a cigarette in the lobby while the fellow entered his office and spoke over the phone. I had the vague feeling of being about to wake up from a deep, numbing sleep. Everything was just as I remembered it: wooden benches, handwritten signs, the huge clock with arrow-pointed iron hands. Ten minutes to eleven.

"He'll be here any moment," he told me from his office, "but you're better off waiting inside. The rain's just started and it'll be a drencher. Pity the turnip who has to spend tonight out in the open!"

After fifteen years in Madrid the expression surprised me, but when the man gazed at me with his small, black eyes, which seemed to have been pasted on beside the red, bulbous nose that rose above his wide, Franco-inspired moustache, there was nothing for it but to laugh at his witticism. Then, without a further word between us, he left me alone in the lobby.

I sat down on the bench nearest the door, after glancing out of the window to check that the road was still empty, and was suddenly overcome by an irresistible desire to flee, to go anywhere, to stay in that station only until the next train came, no matter where it was going, and avoid the inevitable disaster that awaited me in Villasanta. I knew it had been crazy of me to think that in a town this size, no matter how much it might have grown or how modern it might have become, I could avoid running into Celia, who even now must be sleeping in the wide iron bed where we first made love, where I first saw her naked body, the body that still appears in my dreams, which now, in her sixty-seventh year, must be withered and wrinkled as a wilted flower. What would I say when I saw her? What would she say to me? Maybe she would pretend she did not recognize me and walk right past, as proud and straight as ever, her head like the head on an ancient coin, staring into the distance as if peering into some other world. Maybe she had forgotten the love and the pain of those months twenty-five years ago. Maybe she would greet me warmly, with cordiality, not hatred or trembling rage. Maybe she had married some widowed notary who, at the end of his life, had let her taste the unknown pleasure of being the legitimate wife of a man she did not have to be ashamed of. Because, when I knew her, she was what my parents called "a marked woman".

When they had found out that I was hanging around her, Mamá had told me her story. Celia was about her age, or a bit younger; in their youth they had both worked in Doña Laura's workroom, sewing their wedding trousseaus, though Celia wanted to be a dressmaker and her boyfriend did not like the idea of her working after they were married. One day a stranger showed up in town, a mysterious man, Mamá said, an outsider who appeared from out of nowhere, whom no-one knew; a well educated and elegant older man, who drove Celia wild within a matter of days. Celia left her boyfriend without bothering to give a reason, and for the next few months she was seen everywhere arm in arm with the stranger – quite a scandal back then – ignoring the opinions of her widowed mother, her girlfriends, the neighbours, and all the fine, upstanding people who feared for her reputation. She defied everyone for his sake, and with him she laughed at them all, announcing their wedding in the church of Santa María on the first Sunday in December. And then the inevitable occurred, just as everyone in town had feared or hoped. On her wedding day, when she was ready, dressed in white and waiting only for the honeysuckle bouquet that was the groom's to bring, the stranger never turned up. They never heard from him again, though later on it was said that the dollars he had exchanged in the bank were counterfeit. He disappeared just as he had come, and no man ever got close to her again, because everyone in town knew that a girl who had allowed her fiancé to touch her in public – a fiancé in his forties, with an unknown past, who disappeared on the day of the wedding – could never have maintained the chastity that she would have needed if a decent Villasanta boy were ever to enter into a formal relationship with her.

"I think she's still waiting for him," Mamá said when she finished her tale. "She's rebuilt her life to a certain extent, I know. She's travelled abroad, she's read a lot, she makes dresses that all the finest shops in the city want to get their hands on, but she's never found a man like the one she lost. And I think, in her heart of hearts, she is secretly still waiting for him. That woman isn't for you, son. Apart from the fact that she's old enough to be your mother, she is already taken. And if you set your heart on something that can never be, it'll kill you."

We never spoke of her again – not even after she left me, not after I moved away from Villasanta without explaining why, not when I refused to study highway engineering in Montecaín and chose instead to take up Uncle Eloy's offer to let me help out in his watchmaker's shop until I could settle down and decide what I wanted to do with my life. I had nothing to decide. I was like a wounded warrior, a boy who finds himself missing a leg or permanently blind at the age of twenty. Celia had wrenched something from me that I have never been able to name but that I nonetheless know was vital to being a complete man. I had no choice but to accept it and to learn to live with it, eschewing melodrama, avoiding tragic theatricality. When someone loses a hand to a mechanical saw, he learns how to manage with his other hand, until he gets to a point where he barely misses it, although the stump is always there to remind him of his slow reflexes, his clumsiness, the fateful mistake that turned him irreversibly into what he is now. I have never been one for self-pity. What I lost was partly made up for by what I gained: my solitude, my love of a job well done, the manual dexterity that I began discovering at Uncle Eloy's workshop, first by repairing watches, then the odd bracelet, until bit by bit I entered into the fascinating world of gems and jewellery design that would ultimately become my passion and my calling.

That night, in Negresco's, Celia kept shooting me mysterious, sidelong glances, as if she had been captivated by my eyes in some way that I dared not believe, as if she were looking for something in me other than myself. Her glances increased my inner awareness of the looming disaster, because what she was looking for could not be me. Me, a boy of nineteen, beating his brains out to finish his college entrance prep course, with hardly a notion in the world of what his future life would be; a tall, skinny kid in jeans and a leather jacket, who had never seriously dated any girl.

I watched her torture a napkin in her delicate hands until, taking advantage of her girlfriend's momentary absence, she took a scrap of paper from her handbag and rapidly scribbled a note, only to tear it to pieces and toss it in the ashtray before her friend returned and they both departed. I went to the table where they had been sitting and gathered the torn scraps of paper, fine as confetti, making sure my friends weren't watching. Abruptly taking leave of them, I followed the two women through the centre of town, hiding in doorways and dark shop windows, until I saw Celia disappear into a house on Campoamor Street, number 77. Then I ran off like a thief and in the solitude of my room spent an eternity piecing together the note, written in a cramped, nervous hand:

Come and see me at my house at 1.30. Celia.

It sounds stupid now to say that my head swam, that for several moments I felt as if my room was swelling and shrinking as in my most fevered dreams, that an unknown fear assailed me, that I would have given anything never to have seen her leave the cinema, never to have met her amber gaze.

The black widow. An older woman. Asking a boy to an assignation. At her house. After midnight.

It was almost one. Half an hour to decide whether I dared keep the assignation, which had never truly been posed, or lie in bed and forget everything, which added up to nothing:

a mature, experienced woman had noticed the impression she had made on a tall, skinny boy, and had decided to lure him, in the most soap opera-ish way possible, into a meaningless fling.

The honking of a car horn cut through the rain, dispelling my memories and forcing me to look out of the station window. I saw a taxi driver waiting for me in a big, pot-bellied cab that looked like a relic from some black-and-white movie. I hoisted the pair of suitcases into the back seat and sat in front next to the driver, who smelled like a wet dog.

"Hotel or boarding house, sir?"

"To the Hotel Sandalio," I heard myself say.

I did not know whether or not the Hotel Sandalio, which had fascinated me as a child, was still there, but I decided to take a chance on it that night, when my decisions made no difference because everything had already been decided from the outside, by some other power that was aware of things I could not know. For years the Sandalio was the only hotel in the area, the only one with the right to post the single star that it flaunted proudly on its front door; the magical lodging for travelling theatrical companies, for men passing through on business, for the families of any young man who might come to marry some young Villasanta woman. Its threshold was one that we, the boys of the town, could never cross, because Dimas behind the reception desk made it his job to keep us from pestering the hotel's gentlemen clients, at whom we gaped through the lobby windows. The idea of walking through that vestibule, past its gilded mirror, and up its worn crimson-carpeted steps filled me now with such satisfaction that I felt it would have been worth returning to Villasanta just for this.

"What a night, eh?"

Rain was falling in curtains on the taxi's windscreen. Now and again a streak of lightning would light up the darkness with its violet glow, the dark growing all the deeper as the lightning faded. The whole way there, no other cars crossed our path. I thought there must have been a black-out, for there were no street lamps lit, and the ruins of the castle, which I recalled being lavishly floodlit, were mere shadows against the deeper gloom of night.

The taxi stopped in front of a door from which leaked out a muted light. There was no illuminated sign.

"Hold on a mo, sir, I'll help with that."

Braulio stepped from the car and began lugging down my old leather suitcases, while I took shelter in the doorway and searched my wallet for the taxi fare. Just then another man came running from the hotel, hurriedly putting on his jacket as he did so.

"Braulio, bless your dear heart, you're a godsend. You've got to take me to the hospital in Los Altos. Lolín's about to give birth. You, you can pay him tomorrow," he added without looking my way. "Just fill out the form at the desk, please, and pick whichever room you prefer. Keys are in the cubbyholes. But the best room is number 22. Make yourself at home, sir," he concluded, slamming the door behind him.

A few seconds later, Braulio and the father-to-be were gone, swallowed by the storm, and I found myself alone in the lobby of Hotel Sandalio.

Everything was just as I remembered it from childhood: the little ornate mirror like a prop borrowed from some amateur theatre company; the black iron handrails decorated with small iron flowers; the deep crimson carpet; the mysterious depths of the lobby, barely touched by the bluish light of the oil lamp that burned on the reception desk; the gilded keys in their cubbyholes; the silence, dense, almost tangible, like the silence of a church.

I approached the desk and had begun to fill out a form, leaning my elbow on the open registration book, when my eyes drifted to the right of the blank card and, almost without my realizing it, scanned the birth dates of the other guests: 1922, 1917, 1924, 1911. My pen remained suspended in midair, hovering over the form. The youngest person here would be seventy-five years old. The hotel must have been converted into an old people's home since I had left Villasanta, and the taxi driver must have thought I was coming to visit one of the residents. There was no other way to explain why he had not told me.

I left the form unfilled and grabbed the key to room 22, planning to stay only the night, though I had a fleeting impulse to go to my former home and forget about the hotel. But I quickly understood how absurd it would be to traipse halfway across town in the pounding rain and take shelter in a house where no-one had lived for more than twenty years, simply because I did not feel like sharing a presumably comfortable hotel with a handful of old people.

When I looked out of the window of my room, the street remained dark and empty, the rain against the pavement making a tapping noise that was calmingly familiar, and when I climbed into the cold, damp sheets, for a moment I felt transported to my childhood, window to my right and night table to my left, mirrored wardrobe in front, rain falling imperturbably on the tiled roofs, and wonderful dreams on the way.

On the night of my assignation with Celia it did not rain and my dreams were not lovely. In the worst nightmare I have ever had, one that it has taken me a quarter of a century to understand, I saw myself stepping down from one train only to climb on to another, and then another, in a vast station with high-vaulted glass ceilings where all tracks criss-crossed, forming a labyrinth, while a man in a dark uniform, with no face or eyes, wearing a huge black cap like a crown on the blank slate of his head, asked me in his strident voice, "Where do you want to go? Where do you want to go?" and I, sweating in my dream and trying to see what was happening around me, fighting to hold my eyelids open though they felt heavy as stones and kept slipping over my eyes and hiding from my sight the face of Celia, just barely visible behind the glass of a train window, answered with an effort, "Back, back." But the word refused to leave my lips and the man forced me on to a train heading in

30

the wrong direction, while Celia receded from me, her face contorted into a grimace of inconsolable grief.

The next morning I called myself an imbecile and a coward through all my classes. I tried to think of a way to see her, to speak to her, to do something to be by her side; no matter that she was an older woman and I little more than an adolescent. Nothing occurred to me. I knew where she lived, but I could not just show up there without an excuse that would allow me to retire with dignity if she did not want to have anything to do with me.

I was already walking home, going over all the outlandish tales I had seen in the movies about how to approach a woman, when a girl from my classes stopped me to ask whether I would take part in the church collection drive for overseas missions on Sunday. I was about to tell her to get lost, that I had better ways to spend my Sunday mornings, when it suddenly occurred to me that this might be the solution: show up at Celia's house early, but at a reasonable hour, with the excuse of collecting money for the poor black people in Africa. Needless to say, this was a stomach punch to my poor nineteen-year-old self-esteem, but it was also a possible beginning for something that I found too important to be denied by considerations of manly pride. I told her she could count on me, and we agreed to meet at 9.00 a.m. in front of Santa María's.

But it was not necessary. Almost as soon as I came home for lunch, Mamá told us we would have to manage dinner on our own as best we could that night, because she was going to the movies with a group of girlfriends to see the revival of *Gone with the Wind*, the top film of her youth.

"We've agreed to meet for supper at the club, and then we'll go to the cinema to cry ourselves silly for four hours straight."

I do not know why my mother always said "cry ourselves silly" as if she thought that was the finest pleasure the cinema had to offer.

"Who's going?" my father asked.

"The usual group, plus Celia and Amalín, just like old times."

"The fearsome seamstresses of Doña Laura's workroom," he added, smiling at the memories.

Suddenly my mouth went dry, and I had to put down my fork to keep them from seeing how badly my hand was trembling. It is curious how clearly I remember the scene, but if I close my eyes I can still see the Formica-topped kitchen table, the Duralex plate, the fork from the everyday cutlery sitting there like a metallic butterfly, reflecting the two o'clock sun, my own hand with its long, skinny fingers which, over the years, would grow strong and skilful but which at that moment had never yet caressed the creamy skin of Celia.

"Can I go with you, or is it women only?" I asked, to my own surprise.

My father was bemused. "Since when did this sort of thing interest you?"

"I don't know. I've heard so much about that film, I'd like to form my own opinions about it."

"Can I go, too?" asked my sister.

My mother seemed rather proud. "Let's all go, if you'd like. But not to supper. That's only for the girls from the seamstress workroom. No kids allowed there."

The film was at eight. At a quarter past seven, Carmina and I queued up in front of the cinema door, holding a spot for our mother and her girlfriends. I had the sensation that I would faint when I saw Celia.

I never got the chance. When they finally arrived, like a flock of pigeons attracted by a fistful of rice, Celia was not with them. I had to bite my lips to keep from asking where she was; fortunately, one of my mother's acquaintances, who had been waiting in the queue near us, asked instead. That way I discovered that Celia had gone to the train station to pick up a package and would be coming straight to the cinema.

We occupied two rows of seats, and Mamá whispered into my ear, "Hold a seat for Celia. The place is packed, and if I save her a seat I'll feel forced to give it up."

Five minutes after the film started, she arrived. They waved and pointed her to her seat. I picked up my jacket, and for a second our eyes met. I have no idea what happened on the screen for the next four hours. I have fleeting memories of a flame-filled sky, of two profiles, one dark and the other pale, of a large white house. Nothing else. All my memories are centred on the electric sensation of Celia's body next to mine, separated from me only by the armrest; the round pallor of her knees, her hands, pressed together as if in tortured prayer; tears streaming down her right cheek, dried with an antique handkerchief, and an old-fashioned scent, as if of violet water, emanating from her body when she shifted in her seat.

When we left, all the women smiling and with reddened eyes, Celia had to stop at the food stand to pick up that package, which they had been holding for her while the film was on.

"Let's see," said one of my mother's friends. "Isn't there some young gentleman here who can carry Celia's package home for her? It must weigh a ton." She was staring openly at me.

I stammered something that must have sounded like assent, and someone placed the package, like a gigantic child, in my arms, blocking my view of Celia's figure as she walked ahead and paid no attention to me, a white goddess followed by her porter through some mysterious labyrinth. In this fashion I climbed three flights of a narrow, dark staircase after her, resting on the landing while she unlocked the door with an enormous key, then pointed me to the console table where I was to set down my load, and shut the door behind us.

We stood there in the vestibule, gazing at each other, scarcely able to see in the dark flat, lit only by the light of a street lamp that filtered through the balcony window. She pulled off her gloves, very slowly, breathing rapidly as if climbing three flights of stairs had been an uncommon effort.

"Who are you?" she asked me in a trembling voice.

"Marga's son," I answered.

"Go on, run along. It's late. Thank you for . . . ."

I could not reply; it was as if an invisible hand were strangling me. This woman attracted me in a way I have never been able to understand; it was as if she had speared me with a harpoon and was amusing herself by letting out the line and then pulling it taut again, while the iron dug its way deeper and deeper into me. But she was not enjoying it. There was suffering in her expression, as if she could not bring herself to let me go, as if she too felt the bite of the harpoon that was killing me.

I passed her without looking at her, heading towards the door that stood behind her. She raised a hand, whether to say goodbye or to stop me I do not know, and her fingers came level with my temple, perhaps involuntarily, and caressed my face. I felt an electric shock that almost blinded me, but I did not step aside. Little by little, with exasperating slowness, her hand slid down my cheek, brushed back up, twirled my hair, slipped down to my lips, which could not help but form into a kiss that I was already about to regret when she took a step towards me, and suddenly her mouth was where her fingers had been a second before.

I do not know how long we kissed there, in front of the closed door, in the darkness. A length of time no clock could measure, a time not of this world.

"You've come back, my God, you've come back," I heard her murmur. I did not understand, and it did not matter. The only thing that mattered to me was holding her in my arms, feeling her body, her desire, the miracle I had never dared to hope for.

We kissed again, a long, desperate kiss, as if in farewell, not a fresh beginning. Then she stepped away from me, panting, leaned against the door for a moment, and threw it open.

"It's late. Marga will be waiting up for you."

I wanted to tell her it did not matter, tell her to let me stay with her, if only for one more kiss, but I did not dare. I bowed my head and crossed the threshold without asking her when or how we would see each other again, whether she wanted us to see each other again.

Before shutting the door she murmured, in a voice so low I almost had to imagine her words, "Tomorrow is Saturday. Make something up and come and see me tomorrow night, at" – she paused for what seemed an eternity – "eleven. No. At ten. If you want to. I've been waiting so long for you..."

The door closed and I went home in a daze, walking like a puppet, like the robot on a string I was given when I was eight, one foot stepping after the other, not knowing where I was going, until at some point I found myself in my own bed, nodding off and waking up every few minutes, fearing that it had all been a dream, that Celia had never returned from the station and that her kisses and her message had been only a mirage.

That was also how I slept that first night in the Hotel
Sandalio: in and out, intermittently awakened when the bells
of Santa María tolled the hours, when the rain stopped at
some point before dawn, leaving a void, a kind of hole in the
night, filled with a sudden, doughy silence, feeling myself
defenceless against an undetermined danger. I awoke disori-
ented, not knowing where I was, thinking at times that
I was in my childhood bedroom, that if I called out, my
mother would come in and place her hand against my
brow and ask me what was wrong. I realized after a few
moments that I was a full-grown man, lying in a bed in
the Hotel Sandalio, on a woollen mattress with a trench-like
dip in its centre; a man who ought to have gone on to
Oneira and said goodbye to Uncle Eloy, who ought to be
figuring out how to while away the time until his plane
took off, yet who, on some ridiculous whim, was here in
Villasanta, about to spend an entire morning contrasting

his moth-eaten memories with the present. Having come to terms with reality, I fell asleep again.

I got up early, at the first light of day, and went to the antediluvian bathroom to shave with cold water. I thought that I would take a walk round the town and contemplate the ravages that time must have wrought on Villasanta, taking stock as I shaved of what time had done to my own face: slight bags under the eyes, grey hairs everywhere, eyes once bright, now opaque, like river pebbles plucked from the water. What would my town be like? Tricked out in modernity, like all the rest, full of spanking new buildings in place of the old two-storey houses with their balconies and their front doors left always ajar? With hypermarkets, bingo halls and cafeterias, with video shops instead of the huge cinemas of my youth, which would have been replaced by the little boutique multi-screen cinemas that modern mayors are always so proud of? What would be left from my time that I might still recognize? Would Celia's house still be there? Would I dare return there, if only to pass her door and remember? Would I be brave enough to look up her name in the phone book, ring her, invite her for a cup of coffee after twenty-five years of practising to forget her, and confess to her that I had failed?

I put on the same suit I had worn the day before, the one I had decided to wear for saying goodbye to Uncle Eloy, who had always been a fan of strictly conservative clothes. I had thought that I would give the old man a bit of joy before I left for New York to start a new stage of my life designing jewellery for the American women who, a few years earlier, thanks to Madeleine and her tastefully upmarket shop, had discovered my somewhat old-fashioned, vaguely modernist style. Now, suddenly, I saw myself looking more disguised than ever in my dark grey suit, striped tie, and blue raincoat – my modest homage to Cohen. Like a traveller from another era. But I was too lazy to open my suitcase and rummage through my things for jeans and a sweater. I did not think I would be staying long enough to bother undoing my bags; my idea was to leave that very afternoon and reach Oneira in time for supper, which Uncle Eloy would insist on paying for, in whatever restaurant was enjoying his temporary approval.

I walked downstairs to the reception, careful not to make any noise. Old people are light sleepers, and it was barely after seven. I still needed to pay for the hotel room and the taxi that had brought me here, and I wanted to visit Negresco's to see if they served cream pastries for breakfast as they used to do, before I took off on the long stroll around all the sites of my memories.

Standing in front of the desk was a man of my age – moustache, crew cut, also dressed in a suit – who greeted me as soon as he heard me coming down the stairs.

"Good morning! Do you happen to know where Dimas has got himself to?"

The name made me smile. Perhaps old Dimas had wanted to relive his exploits by giving his name to his son, the very son who had become, just a few hours ago, father to a new Dimas, tiny and unaware of his fate.

"I don't know if we're talking about the same one," I replied, "but when I got here last night, he was on his way to the hospital because his wife was having a baby."

"Ah, at last! Poor girl was way overdue, the kid couldn't make up its mind whether or not to enter the world." He slapped both hands against the desk. "Anyway, I have to go, so I suppose I'll just have to leave the money in the till with a note. One never knows how long these things will take, and I have to be in Montecaín tonight after seeing five clients."

He took out his wallet and, to my surprise, pulled from it a five-hundred peseta note, one of the blue notes I recalled from my childhood, though I had not seen one in years. I was about to ask him whether he would let me have a look at it when my eye fell on the calendar that hung on the back wall of the side office.

"Excuse me," I asked, my mouth suddenly dry. "Do you know what today's date is?"

"September the eleventh."

That was true. But what year? That was the real question, but it would not quite emerge from my mouth. Because, if the calendar was not simply a decoration, the large numbers above the page for September said 1952. And that was impossible.

In spite of the old-model taxi that had brought me to the hotel, the lack of street lighting the night before, this man's moustache style and suit, in spite of the calendar and the blue peseta note, it was impossible.

"Well" – he interrupted the hint of hysteria that was starting to grow inside me – "I'm off. Glad to have made your acquaintance. If you should see Dimas, please ask him to save the same room for me, on the same dates next month, and tell him the money's in the till."

No sooner had the man left than I opened the drawer, pulled out the note he had written and contemplated the blue peseta note until its outlines began to blur before my eyes. Then I looked at his signature: Jesús Martín, I was able to make out beneath a florid flourish in fountain-pen ink. I searched through the register and there he was: Jesús Martín, born in Rohíno on 19 April 1917.

The man I had just been talking to was, therefore, eighty-two years old. Assuming it was still 1999, which was no longer clear.

I left the hotel with an unfamiliar sense of anguish crushing my chest. On the street where the Sandalio stood, nothing had changed. Or everything had. It all depended on your point of view. Compared to my childhood, nothing had changed. Compared to my youth, the changes were striking: the street lamps that had been installed when I was twelve were not there yet, but rather at every intersection and in the middle of every block there was a cable from which dangled a naked light bulb, as I vaguely recalled them from my earliest days. There were no parked cars; the door of the single-storey building at the corner of the High Street, where, when I was a teenager, there had been a pharmacy that stayed open on Sundays, was now the entrance to a private house.

My footsteps rang hollow against the pavement, damp from last night's rain. San Onofre Plaza was empty, except for the statue of the saint at its centre, and shrouded in fog. All the shops crowding together under the neoclassical arches of the arcade that lined the plaza had been transformed into padlocked, grey-shuttered hovels. The High Street stretched out in a long, straight line of glass-covered balconies, interrupted only by the proud wrought-iron gate of the club, covered in ivy and climbing honeysuckle. Not a single block of flats, not one garage, not one litter bin.

The desolate emptiness of the plaza convinced me that this must be a dream, and precisely for that reason I did not want to wake up. If my mind was putting on for my benefit the spectacle of an era nearly lost in the depths of my memory, I should enjoy it as long as it lasted, without stopping to think about it; nevertheless, the vapour rising from my breath in the cold morning air, the rumbling of my stomach, and the smell of burning wood stoves that had begun to fill the plaza seemed to be going out of their way to convince me that, for a dream, the clarity and intensity of my perceptions were a little excessive. I usually dreamt in colour, but I had never noticed smells in my dreams, nor had my stomach ever rumbled like this.

A few minutes later, the emptiness lifted like a fog, and groups of people began to walk through the plaza:

schoolgirls linked arm in arm, their hair combed straight and their skirts narrow and long; workers in corduroy trousers and hand-knit sweaters, rushing to get to the factory on time, lunch boxes tucked snugly under their arms, men in peasant berets and sheepskin jackets. Now and again, a well-dressed gentleman tapped the brim of his hat in greeting to some woman who was off to market with a basket on her arm or, with a cardigan spread over her shoulders, held her purse tightly in one hand and carried bread in the other in one of those cloth bags embroidered with cross-stitching, the ones that the girls in our class had to sew while my mates and I were out playing football in the open field that used to face our school.

There was something disquietingly cinematic about the scene, as if all those people had rushed outside for my sole benefit, to convince me of the reality of my situation, as if the fog were being manufactured by some silent machine that had been carefully hidden in the basement of one of the buildings around me, as if the sun that was beginning to redden the rain-slick roof tiles were some gigantic projector designed to give off just the right degree of light.

I planted myself on the corner opposite San Onofre's

statue, like a disciplined tourist who does not want to miss any of the attractions that might cross his path, and stood there for quite a while, gazing spellbound at that nonexistent world.

Everyone stared at me as they walked past – the men discreetly, glancing in my direction with studied nonchalance and quickly turning away, the women more openly, especially the young women, who walked away giggling and nudging each other, and sometimes using any excuse to turn their heads and get another peek. I had never been so aware of how marked the social classes could be, of how easily you could tell who was a worker, who an office clerk, who a common housewife, who a lady from a wealthy family. My head was starting to spin and my feet were freezing as I stood on the corner where I had finally understood what I was: an intruder, a stranger in Villasanta.

I had always felt that I did not fit in, in spite of my family's love, the three or four close friends I had in secondary school, the owners of the shops where my mother always sent me on errands, who used to greet me and ask me about my studies and about the girlfriends I never had. Even at my favourite times, secluded in the municipal library where I sat dreaming about my splendid future until Doña Rosario turned off the lights at ten o'clock and shooed me out, my only desire had been to escape Villasanta and go away to some place that I could feel part of, some mythical land like Samarkand or Paris or, in my more modest phases, Madrid, or even just Oneira. That is something I have never managed to do. I was not happy in Oneira, nor in Madrid, nor do I think I will become happy in New York, especially now, after all that has happened.

And yet, on the day when I woke up after Celia's kiss, I thought I had achieved it, thought that if I had never felt at home in my own skin it was because I had always expected to attain my desires by finding the right place, rather than the right person. "Celia is my home," I thought that morning. "The woman destined for me." Had she not said it herself? "I've been waiting so long for you." The moment had arrived that I had never been able to imagine. The finger of God had touched me.

That day, in literature, the teacher – an enthusiastic fellow barely out of university who was determined to share with us everything that he found exciting – brought us Neruda's *Twenty Poems of Love*. On any other occasion those verses might have made me laugh, but on that day they nearly brought me to tears, right there in the middle of class. Even today, a quarter of a century later, I can recite Poem XVI by heart. But it was the twentieth poem that came to mark my future. Poem XX, "The Song of Despair". I did not know any of this yet, however. At the time, I thought only of the hours that I had to wait until 10.00 p.m., of the excuses I would give to my friends, of what I would say at home, of the fact that at eleven o'clock that very night I would belong to someone, for the first time and for ever, and that Celia would be mine.

I close my eyes and the New York snow keeps on falling outside my window, while my mind fills with disjointed memories of that night, memories frayed around the edges like the pages of a treasured book: Celia trembling, Celia naked, Celia open like a magnolia, crucified by passion on her wrought-iron bed, Celia crying, kissing me, teaching me to love her slowly, to kill her and revive her and destroy her again.

Those were the three most beautiful months in my life, in spite of our quarrels, in spite of the secrecy, in spite of having always to hide our movements so that people would not see us. I wanted us to go everywhere together, but she refused. I suggested going to a hotel in Montecaín so that we could be together without being afraid of the gossip that worried her so much, a fear which I put down to her fascist education among the nuns. She was terrified by the simple idea of taking a train and travelling the thirty ridiculous kilometres that separated us from temporary freedom. I wanted us to marry. She laughed in my face and told me to forget it, it would never happen. "Never," she repeated over and over again until I walked out on her, closing the door carefully behind me to avoid the loud slam that might have put an end to our love. Those were the only real three months in my life, because all the rest, the years before and the years after, have also been life, but muted, in a minor key, like a film with the sound turned down until everything comes out like a whisper, and with colours diluted into sepia tones, into black and white. But I do not complain. Others have had less. I had those three months, and the last three, the months of my return to Villasanta, which began that cold morning in Negresco's magnificent new café, with its recently installed mirrors and its velvet upholstery without a single stain.

I sat at the far table and was about to order a coffee and a cream pastry, enjoying the quiet and excited by the idea that I could read a newspaper from two years before my birth, when I realized that I had no money to pay for it. All this might well be nothing but a dream, but if my money was worthless I could end up in my dream confessing my situation to a pair of Franco-era Civil Guards, and that was enough to scare me, dream or not. So I hurried out of the café, went back to the hotel, opened the drawer, and appropriated the five-hundred peseta note.

When I paid with it, still frightened of what might happen, a very young Fabián put his hands to his head and told me he could not change such a large note, so why did I not go to the bank and come back later to pay him. That gave me the crucial idea. American dollars had not changed in the past hundred years, and if this was really the Spain of the 1950s, nobody would turn up his nose at changing a few hundred dollars for a traveller.

I went to the bank, but after debating whether they could do such a transaction for someone who carried no form of identification, they profusely begged my pardon and asked me to come back with an identity card or a current passport. I left the bank not knowing what to do, sat on a bench in Magnolia Plaza, and began mulling over the matter. The first thing that occurred to me was that I could try to pass as my father, but I immediately realized that in a town the size of Villasanta everyone would know my father, quite apart from the fact that, if this really was 1952, my father would be twenty-seven years old, eighteen years younger than me. I also thought of my paternal grandfather, who had died shortly before I was born and would now be about seventy; then I ran through the names of all my uncles until I remembered that my great-uncle Pablo, my grandmother Dora's brother, had died in Pamplona in 1950. When I was a child my grandmother had always been showing us the old papers she kept in a tin box in the living room cupboard, next to the old family photos and Grandfather Román's medals.

If I went to her house now and managed to get in somehow, I could take Uncle Pablo's identity card. He was not from Villasanta; my grandmother had moved here from Rohíno after she got married. By the end of the day, I would have a suitable date of birth and name. My grandmother had seven brothers; it was unlikely that anyone would be keeping track of which were alive and which were dead, as we were in the depths of the post-war years and there were people still unaccounted for.

I felt an unfamiliar discomfort when I entered my grandmother's house, which I could barely remember from my earliest childhood, because in the month when I took my first communion they tore it down to build a block of flats; but at the same time, along with that nervousness, I was seized by a peculiar elation, as if I had been dead for half a century and had just come back to life.

The door was ajar behind the lowered curtain, as I knew my grandmother habitually left it. She would have gone to the market or the bakery. Regardless, I stood at the doorway and called, "Ave Maria! Anyone at home?" No answer came, and after waiting several seconds I pushed the door open and walked in.

I vividly recalled the geometric floor-tile pattern that sometimes still springs to mind, but I thought that the door to the living room was on the left and was mistaken: it was her bedroom to the left. The living room was directly in front, with its two wing chairs and the enormous radio cabinet that presided over the space like a sultan on his throne. In two strides I crossed over to the small cupboard with green glass doors, opened the drawer, and found there the box full of photographs and documents of the dead, some that I recognized, some unknown to me. My heart was beating like a pneumatic drill, and much as I would have loved to sit in one of those chairs and leaf calmly through the photographs, I knew that every second I stayed was an added risk, so I took out the identity card of my uncle Pablo – who, if I remember correctly, had fought on Franco's side – and an instant later was back out through the curtains and half a step from the street.

I ran straight into a girl who was walking in at just that moment, and who looked familiar to me.

"Were you looking for someone?" she asked me in a

slightly fearful tone while looking over her shoulder, as if hoping to find some kind of protection there.

"For Don Javier Orellana, the doctor," I mumbled.

"Oh, of course! No wonder you were confused. He's next door."

"Forgive me, *señorita*," I said, touching the brim of my hat as I had seen other men doing.

My mother disappeared into the house, and I had to lean against the wall for a few moments. My eyes filled with tears, my chest tightened, I found it hard to breathe. If this was a dream, it was damned true to life. That girl was my mother, forty-seven years ago. My mother, aged twenty-two: young, fresh, as pretty as in the old photographs of her, but in living colour and moving, with a crystalline voice that took me back now to my earliest childhood memories of lullabies sung to send me to sleep. I took out my handkerchief and wiped my eyes and my forehead, bathed in sweat in spite of the morning chill, and for a second I thought I would knock on the door with any old excuse just to talk with her again, bathe in her presence, her smile, perhaps hold her hand. But I knew that was madness. In this dream, or whatever it was, I was a complete stranger, at least twenty years her senior.

I would constantly yearn to hug her, to tell her everything that had happened to me, that had happened to us, and she would avert her frightened eyes and think me some madman escaped from an asylum. It was impossible. My mother had died years ago, in the Oneira hospital, consumed by cancer, one of her hands in my father's and the other in mine. That had been the end of her, and what appeared to me now was a mirage born of my yearning, my nostalgia, my peremptory need to see her again, just one more time, before I left Spain for ever. I would have to be happy with that.

I took a couple of deep breaths, trying to regain my composure. She had not recognized me. My own mother had exchanged a few words with me without knowing me, without her heart telling her who this stranger was. A fit of hysterical laughter came over me. Fearing how people might react, I had to disguise it as a coughing fit, right there in Don Javier's waiting room, under the compassionate gaze of half a dozen citizens of Villasanta. Of course she had not recognized me: she was an unmarried woman, and I was a forty-five-year-old stranger.

"Do you have a number?" Carita asked me in her familiar

screech. She had been Don Javier's nurse since time immemorial, and had held me in her wrestling grip through half a dozen vaccinations.

"No, it's nothing serious. I'll come back later."

"This afternoon Don Javier only does house calls to patients in his practice."

"I'll just come back tomorrow, then."

I took one last look around the blue and black tiled entrance hall, with its delicate wooden benches, and went back outside. The dustman was making the morning rounds with his stinking cart pulled by a bony mule. I went to the bank, changed a few hundred dollars, returned to the still empty hotel, returned the five hundred peseta note to the drawer, and left for a stroll around town. The morning fog had lifted, the pavements had been swept, and in the more distant streets – still unpaved – the women's brooms seemed to have sketched palm trees on the ground. Beyond what used to be my school – what would later become my school – the town practically came to an end: what I remembered as a small open space, enclosed at the other end by seven-storey blocks of flats, was widened now into meadows that spread out, green and peaceful, dotted with cattle, all the way to the foot of the mountains. I could not help taking a glance into the ground-floor window of what would be my primary school classroom: more than thirty schoolboys of all ages, wearing white smocks, jammed on to antediluvian benches, chanting the six-times table at the top of their lungs. The front wall bore a gigantic crucifix, a photograph of a young and soldierly Franco, and a brightly coloured map of Spain. When I realized that a couple of boys had discovered my silent espionage, I brushed the brim of my hat in response to the inquisitive gaze of the schoolteacher, a woman unknown to me, and set off for the snack shop to buy myself a honey cake.

Throughout my walk, while one part of my mind was brimming with joy at the sight of places, details, colours that I had thought lost for ever in the bogs of memory, the other part, like a raptor describing circles above its prey, turned again and again around Celia. I could not be certain that I had enough freedom in this dream to decide on my own immediate movements, but if it were so, in case it were . . . should I go and look for her? Would I want to meet Celia, a Celia scarcely past her teenage years, a Celia whom I might not recognize?

I decided to put off my decision, knowing that I would do it, that I could not help but do it, that I had to see her if only from afar, to see with my own eyes what she had been like, what she was like, now when her life was just beginning: a marriageable girl without a past and with her whole future ahead of her.

In Bustamante Plaza – now called Plaza of the Sacred Heart
by decision of the new Franco-era town government, I
guessed – there were not any pigeons yet, but the bandstand
was still there in the centre of the plaza, and under it was still
the little basement bar that I remembered, smelling of wine
and its huge sack of peanuts. I sat on a stool, ordered the
vermouth and Picón that my grandfather thought of as the
height of sophistication, and thought over the hours to
come. If I wanted to catch the plane that would get me to
London and from there to New York, I would have to be at
the airport by dawn the following day. If I chose instead
to give in to the delicious absurdity of the situation, I could
let the plane ticket go and remain for a few more days in
the Villasanta of the 1950s. After all, the worst that could
happen was that Madeleine might have another one of her
fits of hysteria, and it would be a few more weeks before my
jewellery was put on display in the presence of its creator.

What difference did it make? Who ever gets a chance to see what the world was like before he was born?

It crossed my mind that this might be not quite a dream, but rather one of those hallucinations that they say people have when they have spent a long time in a coma, between life and death; it might be nothing but the cinema of my mind, sweetening my final moments on this earth while my body lay enervated in some hospital for the victims of the latest derailment of the Madrid–Oneira Intercity. But curiously, the idea did not bother me one way or the other. It was simply an idea, whereas the reality all around me was tangible and full of perceptions, though the men surrounding me in the bandstand bar might be nothing but ghosts, and my grandfather's favourite vermouth and Picón nothing but a memory dredged up from the darkest depths of my mind.

Now I would have to go back to the hotel, fill out the form again, using my uncle's name, and, if I wanted to stay for a while, see about buying myself some clothes so that I could pass for normal around Villasanta. I could not remember if you could buy clothes in a store in the '50s, or if you had to go to a tailor and order something made to measure, but I thought I would find out about it that afternoon. With the money I had changed at the bank, Pablo Otero was reasonably rich and could allow himself to live like a wealthy man for a few days.

That was when I thought of the earrings. If I remembered correctly, Mariano's jewellery shop was in the alley behind the church of Santa María, and it was the closest thing to an exclusive jeweller's that you could find in the district. I would go there that afternoon and pick out some earrings for Celia, and maybe send them to her anonymously, by post – the first of the surprises that life would bring her.

Mariano was just as I remembered him, but what seemed normal on an older man – the glasses, the baldness, the slack cheeks and pendulous lips – looked unpleasant on a young man, as if he were wearing a rubber mask that stretched and shrank with every smile he directed at the rich stranger who was able to appreciate his best pieces.

"These are the finest ones I have," he said, holding before my eyes a pair of gold-mounted pearl earrings.

"Don't you have anything similar, but like this" – I drew him a quick sketch – "with a Catalán clasp and a small pearl pendant?"

He looked at me, intrigued.

"I'm a jeweller, too." I don't know why, but it did not sound right to tell Mariano that I was a goldsmith.

"Here they usually wear them short. It takes a while for new fashions to reach us. I imagine that in Madrid now they're wearing them like you say."

"I don't really know. I live in New York." It seemed important to me to have the word spread around town, so that no-one would ask about how I had acquired my dollars.

"Well, those fashions won't reach here for at least five or six years – not until they show up in some movie."

"Could I borrow your workshop? Naturally, I will pay you for the trouble, on top of the material."

I knew that Celia liked pearls, and that she kept a pair of earrings in her bedside table drawer that she never let me see, which in my teenage jealousy I identified without any real basis with the old man she had been in love with in her youth. Suddenly, giving her one of my jewellery pieces seemed to me like the only hidden meaning in the madness that was surrounding me.

At eight in the evening, the tiny parcel in my pocket, I was
back at Negresco's for an aperitif before heading to the
club for dinner, which seemed the proper thing to do for a
recently arrived stranger in Villasanta. There were plenty of
empty tables. I went all the way back to the one against the
wall out of sheer inertia. I hung my raincoat on the coat
rack that was installed, Viennese-style, behind my head, and
decided to try a local wine and watch the people who were
passing by on the narrow pavement or coming in for a glass
of red wine before they went home for dinner. A group of
young men caught my eye when they walked in, wriggling
like a pack of dogs to shake off the rain that had just begun
to fall, warm and gentle, almost discreet, the way autumn
rain falls in Umbría. There were five of them. In their twen-
ties, labourers or low-ranking clerks to judge by their cloth-
ing. They were shoving and clapping each other on the back
and laughing at jokes that did not reach the corner where

I sat, reminding me of myself and my schoolmates. By the time I was their age, I no longer laughed or roamed the bars in a pack.

There was something familiar about them, and for a moment I thought they might be the fathers of the same friends I had just been thinking about, still unmarried, still just starting out in life, and that made me feel old, out of place, lonely. Lonely as I had never felt before, despite being long accustomed to it.

I had just decided that I had better pay and get going, when the door opened and in marched a bunch of girls, to judge by their voices, for their bodies were hidden by the pack of men, and at that instant the whole group turned towards the back of the room, towards me, and started walking in the direction of the table where I was sitting. Arm in arm with a girlfriend, her hair combed up into an implausible chignon, wearing a blue dress with a tight-fitting top and flowing skirt, Celia, a very young Celia without mysteries or secrets, looked at me, curious.

I felt as if I had been paralyzed. Celia was looking at me, the others were looking at me, and I returned their gazes, stunned by the magnitude of what was happening to me, while for them it was just a matter of a stranger who had taken their usual table.

"Would you mind switching tables?" asked a boy with reddish blond hair and a kind of porcine look in his small blue eyes. "The thing is, we always sit here, you know? So we don't bother anyone. Since there's so many of us. . . ."

My *déjà-vu* was so strong, I felt that the world had begun to spin around me and that the whirlpool would swallow me in the end. Celia was looking at me, flirtatiously, without recognizing me. How could she have recognized me?

"This is your hang-out, then? Don't worry, I'll find another spot."

The boy yanked my blue raincoat off the rack, ripping a length of the collar seam, to alarmed screams from the girls.

"Oops, so sorry, sir. I've never seen a raincoat with one of these loops for hanging it on a rack, you know."

"It's made in America," I lied, when I was able to speak again.

"Ah, so that's it."

Celia let go of her friend's arm and stepped up. "Hand it

over, clumsy. I'll sew it up, don't you worry."

"Please don't worry about it, *señorita*, it doesn't matter." The words slipped out before I had time to think.

"But it's no trouble at all for me. Anyway, I'm a seamstress – well, nearly a seamstress," she corrected herself, amid her friends' laughter. "Are you staying at the Sandalio?"

"Of course he is," one of the other girls interrupted. "You don't think he'd be staying at Damián and Florinda's boarding house, do you?"

"So, tomorrow I'll bring it to you, good as new. Come on, blockhead," she said, turning to the fellow who had torn my raincoat, apparently her boyfriend, "let's leave this gentleman alone. OK. I'll get it back to you tomorrow. And you're going to pay for his wine, Onofre."

"His glass is on the house." Fabián settled the matter.

I stood up to leave, feeling all the while Celia's gaze on the back of my head while my left hand gripped the inner pocket of my jacket, where the earrings waited in their box. Before I stepped outside, I heard Onofre's voice – "Who do you suppose that chap is?" – mixed with another voice, a woman's voice, asking: "Is Margarita not feeling well, Antonio? She didn't show up at the workshop today."

At that moment I realized that one of those boys was my father, but I did not catch sight of him because the door had just closed shut behind me.

An entire day has gone by. I have been at the workshop that Madeleine found for me, I have eaten lunch with her and her two partners in one of those places for the beautiful people, where all the women look like C.N.N. anchors and all the men wear Armani suits. Wandering around the streets of Midtown, which are decked out for the Christmas and New Year that I will probably spend alone in my empty flat, I have tried to shake off the sense of unreality that has dogged me for the past week. I have not been able to. All day long, I have walked among ghosts: people not yet born, future corpses, souls trapped in their tiny bubbles of time – ninety years if they are lucky – that will pop at any moment, leaving nothing more than a splattering of what was once their essence. I have tried to work myself up to the decision of burning these pages, which cannot be of interest to anyone, and so freeing myself from finishing this tale, whose end I already know, so that I will not have to relive all the scenes that haunt me; but what good will that do, if they are always there, behind my eyelids, ready to leap out at the slightest excuse?

Before going back, I went up to the observation deck of the Empire State Building and spent half an hour gazing out at city lights that twinkled in the cold night air like stars fallen to earth, and remembering Celia, Celia as a young woman, practically a girl, hanging on my words in the little lobby of the Sandalio as I described New York to her, a city I barely knew, telling me that her life's dream was to go up to the deck of the world's tallest skyscraper, just like she had seen it in some film, and have her lover kiss her, up there, with the world at her feet.

The other Celia, the mature Celia of my first memories, had already gone to New York a year before we met. She told me about it one day, in bed, wrapped around me, her head buried in the hollow of my arm, as if she were confessing something shameful: she had gone to the top of the Empire State alone, because her girlfriend suffered from vertigo, and she had waited, as in that film, for a miracle to occur, for *him* to emerge from nowhere and embrace her unexpectedly from behind, put his hands over her eyes, and bring her back to life with his loving kiss. It was the only time she spoke to me of that man. "But it didn't happen," she said. "It was Christmas, it was very cold, everybody was there with their families or their partners. And I was alone. Angelines was waiting for me downstairs in a cafeteria, scared to death that I had left her alone for half an hour in New York, but Angelines was nobody. Afterwards I thought it had been stupid to wait, melodramatic, ridiculous. He must have been over sixty, if he was even still alive. That's when I knew he'd never return. That's when I knew that all I had left was to grow old, that I had no hopes. And then I met you."

I remember my anger then, my impotence, my itching to tell her, "I'll take you to New York and we'll make love on top of the Empire State Building, at night, surrounded by tourists, with all the lights blazing for us." I waited to tell her this until I was saying goodbye, and she threw her head back and laughed until she cried, stroking my hair as if I was some lost puppy. We never mentioned New York again. Yet scarcely two hours ago, there I was, waiting for her like an imbecile, on the lookout for a single woman in a long skirt and pearl earrings, as she had been at Christmas, 1973, to put my arms round her from behind and finally put an end to all our failed chances. But this isn't Umbría. Here, time flies like an arrow, in a straight line, always forward; it never slows down, never gambols, loops, turns somersaults. Here, turning back is impossible.

Spread out before me, all over the table, are twenty-five exquisite pieces: the Celia Sanjuán Collection, to be put on display on the first of January in a small gallery on Fifth Avenue. The collection that I have named after her, because it makes no difference any more. Yellow topazes the colour of her eyes, blue topazes mounted in platinum, freshwater pearls enmeshed in spirals of gold, silver and mother of pearl, onyx and white gold, all of Celia's faces, all her radiance, her mystery, her intensity, concentrated in small, shining jewels for a future that will never be mine. All that is mine now is the past.

We got engaged on All Saints' Day. I had given her the pearl earrings one October night at the door to her building, after she had told me she had just broken up with the boyfriend who had wanted to forbid her to work, who wanted to control her life. We had all gone to the cinema together, five couples, minus Onofre: my parents – my future parents – and their best friends. They were showing *Gone with the Wind*, that terrible tale of misunderstandings and missed opportunities in which love loses and anger wins the day. Celia told me she could understand Scarlett. I have never been able to. But at that moment I understood Celia's tears in 1974, when her own life had turned into living without a purpose, into an affirmation of the independence that had been imposed on her from without. How could I have understood then what was happening inside her, if I was but a nineteen-year-old boy dazzled by her aura of mystery?

Now I know it was impossible. I could not have competed

with myself, just as the young Celia could not compete with the mature Celia. In the Villasanta of the '50s, Celia was one of the prettiest girls in town, to the extent that sometimes when I went to pick her up at the door of her building, my breath caught in my throat and her magnificent youth made me feel ashamed of myself, of my body in visible decline, of my grey hairs, of the wrinkles in my face, and I could hardly believe that she might love me, might desire me. Yet all her youthful beauty was no more than a work in progress, a mere sketch of what I had already come to know twenty-five years before; and, though her body was smooth and firm and her breasts hard, every time that I embraced her, every time that – the two of us hidden in an abandoned farm on the outskirts of town – I entered her, I was constantly making love with the other Celia, the one who had taught me to love so many years earlier, on an iron bedstead, the marked woman, aged and mysterious, who had made me hers for ever.

And yet I was ready to go through with it. Just two weeks ago, everything was ready for our wedding. My parents were married in early November in the church of Santa María la Blanca, and in the vestibule of the sacristy they published our marriage banns. The priest took our documents to issue us our official family register book. We both had new passports, mine under the name of Pablo Otero, which we obtained in record time, thanks to a paternal uncle of Celia's who enjoyed excellent relations with the local police. The girls had been working night and day to finish Celia's trousseau in time for the wedding, in spite of the fact that her mother roundly opposed Celia's marriage to a man who had come from nowhere, a man who gave lavish gifts and said that he lived abroad.

Possibly it was at my parents' wedding that I stopped thinking it was all a dream or a hallucination. All my relatives, those I remembered and many I had forgotten, were there, young, happy, decked out in their Sunday best, so many of them now dead. The banquet – chocolate, pastries, wedding cake – was held in a rented hall. Then they danced *paso dobles*, waltzes, and *jotillas*, while I stared at that parade of ghosts from times past and yearned to shout until I was hoarse, to let my parents know that they would have two children and would be happy for a few years, only to sink into despair over losing Carmina, over having to go to Paris to bring her coffin home, over losing me next in the quicksand of my love for Celia, to the backroom of Uncle Eloy's jewellery shop, where I would turn into a recluse, soul-wounded. I yearned to tell them that Grandmother Dora would grow senile and at last would be confined to her room, raving, for years, confusing past and present, the dead and the living, in a fiendish whirl that would fray my mother's nerves. But how could I tell them? Above all, what for? If I married Celia at the end of the month – I had flatly refused the date that the parish priest proposed, the first Sunday in December – everything might be different. Time would change course like a sailboat buffeted by a gust of wind, and we would all get a new chance, a new path.

"I love weddings," Celia told me when I walked her home that night. "I hate weddings," she told me twenty-five years earlier, when I wanted her to come with me to the wedding of a friend who was hurriedly marrying his fiancée before her pregnancy would become obvious.

But two weeks ago we were going to get married. The atmosphere was stifling in the Villasanta of 1952: all the blinds had eyes, at every balcony window women sat to do their tatting and their tut-tutting, having elected themselves the guardians of public morality. Until we discovered the abandoned farm, we made love in meadows on the outskirts of town, on a frost-hardened field, under trees stripped bare by the oncoming winter, always fearing the sudden appearance of a pair of patrolling Civil Guards and, with them, scandal. In 1952 her mother was still alive and Celia's flat was off limits, except for a cup of hot chocolate on a Sunday afternoon in the little sitting room with the balcony, from which I was once able to catch a glimpse of the iron bed where, twenty-five years earlier, I had surrendered my inexperience to Celia's thirst, Celia, emerging from a severely tailored dress. "It's Mama's bedroom," she whispered now, catching my glance. How could I tell her that I knew that bed, the creaking of its springs, the metallic clank of its headboard against the wall, the night table where she kept her souvenirs? How could I tell it to the clear-faced girl who responded to everything I said with a trusting, possessive smile, to the smooth-bodied, fresh-smelling child who had not yet learned what it means to lose and to desire?

I could have told the other Celia, though she would not have believed me. Grief grants some people the wisdom that innocence denies them. That Celia – her I could have told. But the I who knew the other Celia was a timid boy who had not yet learned about losing love, an unscarred boy who burned in Celia's fire, who quenched her thirst for a few moments, only to make her more ravenous, impossible to sate.

It was five days to the wedding. Antonio, who was to become my father two years later, went with me to the tailor's to pick up my black suit, as if I were getting dressed for a funeral. The gold wedding ring shone on his finger; he still had not learned to treat it as part of his body, still passed the time spinning it with his thumb. Afterwards we went for a vermouth in the bandstand bar.

"Know what?" he said. "At first I was afraid you'd try to take Margarita away from me. You looked at her so often."

"It's because your wife's so good-looking, old boy." He liked hearing that Margarita was now his wife. "But from the very start I knew it was Celia that I loved."

"You two make a good couple. I think young guys don't suit her character. Since she doesn't have a father . . . " He suddenly stopped short when he realized not only that he had called me an old man, but that he thought I was going to be some sort of substitute father figure. I had to laugh.

"You're not planning to play some underhand trick on her, are you? I don't know what you two have already done, not that it's any of my business, but Celia is a good kid and I'd hate it if . . ." He did not finish the sentence.

"Don't worry, old boy. If everything comes off the way I hope, next month we'll be living in New York as man and wife." Over time I had picked up some expressions that I would have been embarrassed to say in my own time.

"As soon as we can save up enough we'll come and visit you."

They never left Umbría, except to go to Paris to bring back Carmina's body. I knew it, and my last sip of vermouth went down bitter.

The next day I had to go to Montecaín to pick up the tickets that a friend of Antonio's had been working to obtain for us. Travel was no easy thing in the post-war years, but with enough patience and friends you could get things. Celia was wild about the idea of the ocean liner that would take us to New York and the aeroplane that we would then take in order to spend a few days at Niagara Falls. She wanted to come with me to Montecaín to pick up the tickets, and we both knew, though we had never said it in so many words, that we would take advantage of the three hours we had before the next train back to hole up in a discreet hotel I had been told about. But we could not go to Montecaín together and risk becoming the talk of the town just days before our wedding, so we decided that she would go on ahead with Margarita, with the excuse of needing something for her trousseau, and then I would catch up with her while my mother made the rounds of the shops. They would take the morning mail train, and I would go later by bus.

I was surprised at how many people were waiting at the bus stop, in the rain, loaded down with baskets and packages tied with string. I was carrying a briefcase to hide the clear plastic handbag that I was planning to give Celia, and all my money, and documents. Back in the room at the Sandalio I had left my wedding suit, which I would see many years later hanging in Celia's bedroom wardrobe, and which she told me had been her father's at his wedding.

I managed to get a seat on a spluttering bus crammed with soldiers and farmhands; I sat down after first offering the place to a couple of little old women in black head-scarves and woollen shawls, who looked at me with incredulity and insisted on standing: "Anyway, we'll be getting off just down the road." I rested my head against the window and, without realizing it, fell fast asleep. Loud laughter and music brought me back to reality.

I had to blink several times to convince myself I was awake. The video system was showing a movie with the sound on at full volume. The other passengers, almost all of them students and well-dressed women, were preparing to get off at the most important university and industrial town in Umbría. The newspaper that someone had left on the seat next to mine said it was 20 December, 1999.

I moved off the bus automatically, on legs that had turned to rubber, feeling the nausea rising in my gut, and, dodging the traffic on Constitution Avenue, I headed for the café where we had agreed to meet, knowing that she would be there, with Margarita, drinking a hot chocolate, waiting for me. Only it would be forty-seven years ago, in a time as far beyond my reach now as the planet Mars.

The café still stood, but it had recently been remodelled and was all metal and glass. The specialities, from Irish coffee to cappuccino, included three different Nepalese teas. A pair of girls sitting at a table stared at me as if they were seeing a ghost. One of them was dark and wore a small pearl in one nostril; on her shoulder, uncovered in spite of the cold, she had a tattoo of a Celtic symbol, the circle of eternal return.

I ran to the train station, took the next train — a nearly empty local — to Villasanta, and tried to fall sleep to force the miracle. I could always tell her that something unforeseen had arisen and that I had not been able to make our date.

I did not succeed. The town where I arrived was the one I had been expecting that September night when time had spun back on itself, a town made ugly by progress, full of street lamps, litter bins, video stores, a town where Negresco's survived, frayed and forgotten, amid modern coffee shops, where the club had lost its garden and had been transformed into a home for old people, widowed and abandoned by their children, where the Sandalio had become a ruin with whitewashed windows: "Coming soon: Tarot Esoteric Books."

I wandered its streets looking for something that could not be there. Don Javier, the doctor, had died many years before, his stately home now occupied by a branch of some bank. Bustamante Plaza had recovered its name but was entirely paved in tiles, filthy with pigeon droppings. My school no longer existed; Carmina's grave displayed the horror of a bouquet of plastic flowers, dusty and broken around the edges. A construction company had begun to demolish the building on Campoamor Street where, that very morning, Celia had dressed for her getaway to Montecaín.

At the train station book shop, while waiting for the Intercity to Oneira, I bought a glossy magazine, *One Hundred Years of Villasanta de la Reina*, published by the town council to commemorate the coming of the new millennium. I felt nothing. It was as if all my insides had been ripped out but the anaesthesia were still keeping the pain under control. I saw people glued to street corners, talking into their mobile phones, and could only think of how easy it was to communicate at the end of the twentieth century. You dial a number and, across a distance of thousands of kilometres, your words ring in the ears of the person awaiting your call: "Sorry, I'll be late," "We'll see each other tomorrow," "I love you."

How could I tell Celia what had happened? How could I put my words in her young, trusting ear? How could I prevent the gibes of Villasanta, the loneliness, the twenty-five years of loneliness and shame that awaited her until I, twenty-five years ago, could come to console her on her loss for a few weeks? If only I had known then, if only I had known what I know now, I could easily have swallowed my youthful pride, have fought for her, even against herself, could have brought her with me to Oneira, lived together with her in the larger town, learned together with her how to squeeze all the juice out of life that is denied to us because we show up at the wrong time. But I did not know. And when she told me, "Go. Go away, for ever," I left.

I did not know then what that youthful love had meant for her; I could not have known that she loved me, that she had always loved me, but with a different body, with a spirit that had been assayed and purified by loneliness, by grief, by time; that the passion she had felt for my nineteen-year-old self had always been defeated in the constant comparisons with her memories of an old man whom I had hated so much, and who was also myself, my other self.

On the plane I leafed through the magazine, pausing at the photographs from the 1950s, looking through the group pictures for anyone I knew. There was a page devoted to the famous Sunday strolls on Jardines Street, where the girls of Villasanta went to show off their boyfriends like thoroughbred dogs. There I found myself, in the double-breasted suit that the tailor had made for me soon after I arrived, in profile, head turned to look at Celia who, in her Sunday dress, the deep crimson one that put colour in her cheeks and that looked dark grey in the photo, exuded pride and happiness from all her pores. The caption read: "Circa 1952. Famous Villasanta dressmaker Celia Sanjuán with an unidentified man." An unidentified man who was now me, with my grey temples, looking aged in my coat and tie, an older man who abandoned a girl at the altar after taking advantage of her. A vulgar, trite, ridiculous tale.

The end pages carried the list of births, marriages and deaths from the last year of the twentieth century. I do not know what led me to look for her name, but there it was: "Celia Sanjuán, dressmaker, 77 Campoamor Street, apartment 3L, died after a long and painful illness in Los Altos Hospital, 1 November, 1999."

My eyes clouded over and it took a nearly impossible effort for me to keep from crying among all those passengers flying to New York to greet the millennium.

I had been out strolling with her while she lay dying in some hospital with no-one to hold her hand, I had been giving her those pearl earrings while she was feeling that her time had run out and that the fiancé of her youth would never come to find her, I had been making love with her while she was being buried in the same cemetery I had visited the day before to take my final farewell of Carmina but where it had never occurred to me to look for her grave, for the grave of Celia.

It has started to snow. The jewels sparkle under the work lamp. Cohen's thick voice trickles like poisoned honey across my memories. I do not wish to continue writing.

Tomorrow is the last day of the century. Tomorrow, wearing my famous blue raincoat, the one that earned me so many sidelong glances in the Villasanta of the '50s and that first led to my meeting Celia, I will go once more to the top of the Empire State Building.

If, apart from Umbría, there is any place and any moment where the impossible can happen, it must be there, tomorrow, at midnight. I will go up to that observation deck where she looked for me on Christmas Day, 1973, and, eyes closed to the snow, the lights, and the fireworks, I will await the miracle.